FREE FALL

FOR KIM
Thanks to Matthew and Daniel

Free Fall

Copyright © 1988 by David Wiesner

Manufactured in China.

All rights reserved.

Library of Congress Cataloging-in-Publication Data

Wiesner, David.

Free fall.

Summary: A young boy dreams of daring adventures in the company
of imaginary creatures inspired by the things surrounding his bed.

[1. Dreams—Fiction. 2. Stories without words.] I. Title.

PZ7.W6367Fr 1988 [E] 87-22834

ISBN 0-688-05584-2 (lib. bdg.) 0-688-10990-X (pbk.)

Visit us on the World Wide Web!

www.harperchildrens.com

DAVID WIESNER

FREE FALL

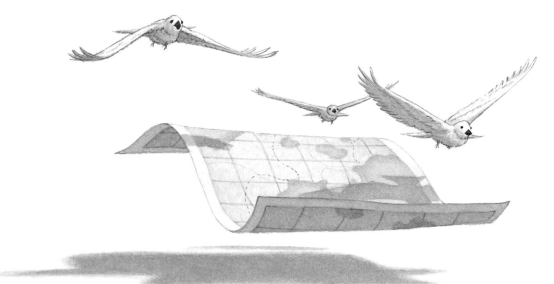

HARPERCOLLINSPUBLISHERS

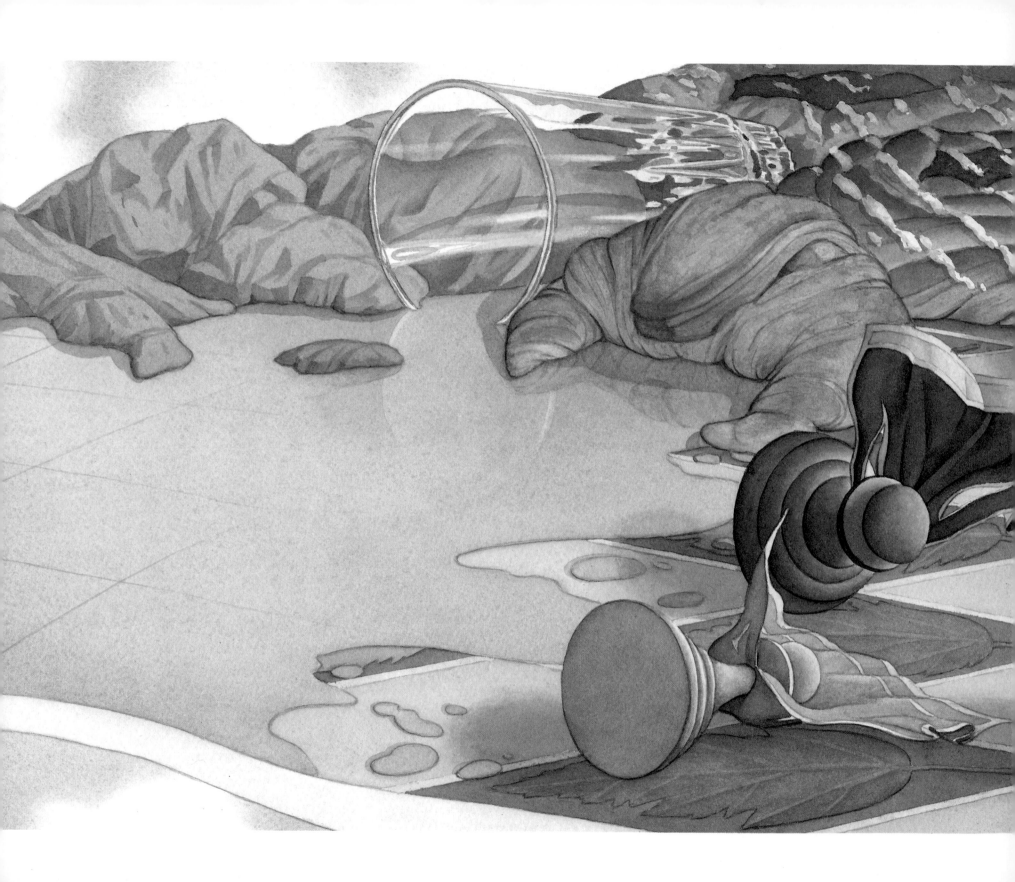

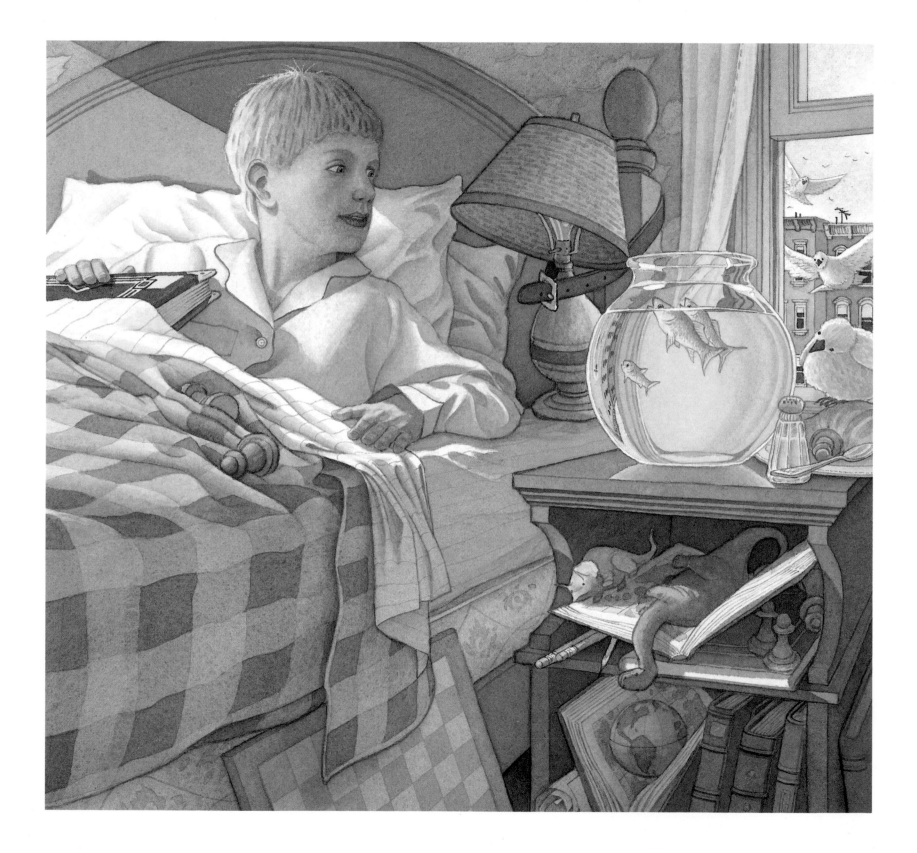